SOPHIE MARLOWE

The Off-Limits Surgeon

A Sweet Enemies to Lovers Billionaire Romance

Contents

One

Scrubbing in on Love

I tug at the hem of my scrubs for the tenth time this morning, trying to smooth out imaginary wrinkles. My heart pounds in my chest, echoing louder than the hospital's bustling corridors. Miami's top hospital. My dream job. And yet, my palms are slick with sweat, and I can't shake the gnawing feeling of nausea in my stomach.

"You've got this, Ava," I whisper to myself, taking a deep, steadying breath. The sharp scent of antiseptic fills my nose, grounding me in this surreal moment. I've worked so hard to get here, sacrificing sleep, weekends, and a social life. Now, it's finally happening.

The OR doors loom ahead, sterile white and intimidating. I swipe my ID badge and push through, immediately greeted by the controlled chaos of the operating room. Machines beep rhythmically, and the overhead lights are blindingly bright. The air is cold—not just in temperature, but in atmosphere. The chill seeps through my scrubs, making me shiver, but it's the icy demeanor of the team that really makes me feel out of place. Nurses and doctors move with practiced precision, their faces hidden behind masks, their interactions clipped and strictly businesslike.

"You must be the new scrub nurse," a voice calls out, pulling me from my thoughts.

I turn to see a woman with kind eyes, her name badge reading 'Linda.'

"I'm Linda, the charge nurse. Stick with me, and you'll be just fine."

I nod, grateful for the warmth in her tone. "Thank you. I'm Ava Martinez."

"Let's get you settled," she says, guiding me to the scrub station. As I wash my hands, I mentally rehearse everything I've learned. *Stay calm, stay focused.*

Minutes later, I'm in the OR, my heart racing as I take in the scene. The patient is prepped, the surgical team is in position. And there, at the head of the table, is Dr. Ethan Cross.

Even with his mask on, there's no mistaking him. His reputation precedes him—the brooding, recently divorced, billionaire heart surgeon known for his brilliance, impossible standards, and the groundbreaking surgical discovery that made him his fortune. Despite his wealth, he continues to work, throwing himself into his career while navigating an emotional custody battle over his daughter.

His hazel eyes, striking against his rich, warm skin, scan the room with military precision. He has broad shoulders, a strong jawline, and an imposing presence that commands attention without him saying a word. His bald head gleams under the surgical lights as he places his surgical cap on, only adding to his striking appearance. There's a quiet authority in the way he holds himself—a man who's worked hard to be at the pinnacle of his field, yet carries the weight of his personal battles on those broad shoulders.

I'm so focused on him that I almost miss Linda's cue to bring the instrument tray closer. My hands tremble slightly as I pick it up, and in my haste, the tray tilts. Time seems to slow as I trip over an exposed equipment wire. The instruments clatter to the floor, the sound echoing like a gunshot in the silent OR.

The room freezes. All eyes are on me.

Dr. Cross's gaze snaps to mine, icy and unforgiving. "What do you think you're doing?" His voice is low, but it carries an edge that cuts deeper than any scalpel.

"I—I'm sorry," I stammer, my face burning with embarrassment. Linda rushes to help, but the damage is done.

"Get her out of my OR," Dr. Cross says sharply, turning back to the patient as if I'm nothing more than an inconvenience.

Linda gently steers me out of the room, her expression sympathetic. "Don't take it personally. He's... difficult."

But her words don't soothe the sting of humiliation. Tears begin to build up in my eyes, and I am reminded that there is no crying in the OR. I lean against the wall, my mind racing. Maybe I'm not cut out for this after all.

As I try to gather my shredded dignity and head to the break room, I hear Dr. Cross's voice through the slightly ajar OR door.

"No, I can't meet today," he's saying, his tone softer but strained. "The custody hearing's next week, and I need more time. She's my daughter. I'll fight for her."

Curiosity flares within me. The cold, unfeeling surgeon has a daughter? And he's fighting for her?

I walk away, my mind swirling with questions I have no right to ask.

I spend the rest of the day trying to shake off the disastrous start. Linda assigns me to shadow another nurse, but my mind keeps drifting back to the OR—and to Dr. Cross. His harsh words replay in my head, each time cutting a little deeper. But it's that conversation I overheard that sticks with me. The way his voice softened when he spoke about his daughter, the raw tension in his words... It doesn't fit with the image of the cold, unfeeling surgeon everyone talks about.

By the time my shift ends, I'm exhausted—mentally and physically. I peel off my scrubs, grateful just to have survived the day without being fired. I gather my backpack and walk through the endless hospital halls, desperate for fresh air. I step outside into the humid Miami evening, letting the heavy warmth thaw the chill that's been settled in my bones all day. As I walk to my car, I tell myself tomorrow will be better. It has to be.

But fate has other plans.

The next morning, Linda greets me with a sympathetic smile. "You're scheduled in Dr. Cross's OR again today."

My stomach drops to my shoes. "Seriously?"

"Seriously. But don't worry," she adds quickly, patting my arm. "Just stay focused. You'll be fine."

Fine. Right. I can do this.

I spend the morning rehearsing every step in my head, determined not to make the same mistake twice. When it's finally time to scrub in, my hands are steady—or at least steadier than yesterday.

Dr. Cross doesn't acknowledge me when I enter the OR. His focus is entirely on the patient, his expression a mask of concentration. But I can feel his presence, the weight of his high expectations pressing down on me like a physical force.

5

The surgery progresses smoothly, and I manage to keep up without any major mistakes. But just when I start to relax, Dr. Cross speaks.

"Martinez," he says, his voice sharp but not as cold as before. "Hand me the clamp."

I move quickly, double-checking the instrument before placing it in his hand. Our fingers brush—a static spark through the latex—and for a split second, his hazel eyes meet mine. There's something there—something intense and guarded that I can't quite read.

The moment passes, and he turns back to the patient, but my heart is racing for an entirely different reason now.

By the end of the procedure, I'm mentally drained but relieved. No dropped instruments, no scathing remarks. Progress.

As we clean up, I catch snippets of conversation from the other nurses. They're gossiping about Dr. Cross, speculating about his personal life—his messy divorce, the custody battle, and how he's still off-limits despite the allure. I try to ignore it, but my curiosity gets the better of me.

Later, as I'm leaving the hospital, I see him in the parking lot, leaning against his luxury car and talking on his phone. His posture is tense, his free hand rubbing his bald head in obvious frustration. I can't hear what he's saying, but the strain on his face is clear even from a distance.

I shouldn't care. I barely know him. And besides, he's completely off-limits—especially to someone like me, a rookie nurse. But something about that look—that raw vulnerability—pulls at me.

As I slide into my car, I pause for a moment, my hands gripping the steering wheel. The logical part of me screams to let it go— to chalk it up to professional curiosity. But deep down, I know it's more than that. There's a story behind those striking hazel eyes, a story I can't ignore.

I start the car but linger for a few moments longer, watching through the windshield as Dr. Cross paces beside his car, still on the phone. His voice rises, sharp with frustration, and though I can't make out the words, the desperation is clear. The man who exudes absolute control inside the OR looks like he's barely holding it together out here in the real world.

I've always believed people are more than the masks they wear— literally and figuratively. And something tells me that beneath Dr. Cross's gruff exterior lies a man battling more than just custody papers.

I put the car in gear and drive home, but my thoughts are still with Dr. Ethan Cross. The man is a puzzle, and I can't help but wonder what it would take to piece him together.

Two

Collateral Heart Damage

The OR has always been my sanctuary—a place where precision and control rule, where emotions are checked at the door, and the only thing that matters is the patient on the table. But lately, even here, I can't escape the chaos my life has become.

I scrub in mechanically, the familiar routine failing to calm the storm brewing inside me. The divorce papers, the custody battle... it's all bleeding into my work. I'm not the surgeon I used to be—focused, untouchable. I catch myself snapping at the nurses, losing my patience over minor mistakes—like I did with that new scrub nurse, Ava Martinez.

I didn't mean to be that harsh, but seeing her fumble in my OR set something off. Maybe it's because she reminds me of a time when I was new, eager... before everything fell apart.

The bright, sterile lights overhead reflect off the gleaming surgical instruments, casting sharp shadows on the walls. The hum of the ventilator and the rhythmic beep of the heart monitor should be comforting—a reminder that life is being preserved—but today, they sound more like a ticking clock counting down to something inevitable.

I glance at the clock on the wall, the second hand sweeping forward with relentless precision. Any minute now, my lawyer will call with updates on the custody hearing. The thought of losing my daughter—of not being there for her every day—is unbearable. She's the only thing that kept me grounded during the darkest days of my marriage's unraveling.

My mind drifts to a memory—a sunny afternoon at the park. Lily was only five, her curls bouncing as she ran ahead of me, her laughter filling the air like a melody I never wanted to forget. "Daddy, catch me!" she'd squealed, and I'd obliged, scooping her up and spinning her around until we were both dizzy with joy. Her smile… it was the light in my life, a reminder of what truly mattered.

But now, that light feels so far away, like a distant star flickering on the horizon, just out of reach.

The OR door swings open, snapping me back to the present. The atmosphere shifts subtly as Ava enters, her posture stiff but determined. The sterile air grows even colder as the seasoned nurses exchange glances, their faces tight with thinly veiled resentment. They're withholding guidance, I realize—afraid she might become indispensable to me. It's ridiculous. I don't

9

need anyone, especially not a rookie nurse. But still... there's something about her persistence, her unwillingness to back down even after yesterday's disaster, that gnaws at me.

The surgery proceeds smoothly, but my mind isn't fully in it. Each incision, each suture feels automatic, as though my hands are working on muscle memory alone. I'm waiting for the call— the one that could change everything.

When my phone finally vibrates against my thigh, a jolt of anxiety shoots through me, sharp and piercing.

I step out of the OR, stripping off my gloves with a snap that echoes down the empty hallway. The stark white walls feel like they're closing in, suffocating me. "Cross here," I answer, my voice low and taut.

"Ethan, it's Mark," my lawyer's voice comes through, calm but carrying an undercurrent of tension. "We've hit a snag. Your ex-wife's lawyer is pushing for sole custody, citing your long hours and... emotional volatility."

I grit my teeth, feeling the muscles in my jaw tighten painfully. "That's a load of—"

"I know," Mark cuts in, his tone sharper now. "But we need to be careful. Any slip-up at work, any sign of instability, could be used against you."

My chest tightens like a vise. The OR, my refuge, now feels like a battlefield on multiple fronts. One mistake, one outburst, and

I could lose Lily.

I disconnect the call, leaning against the wall, trying to steady my breathing. The cool surface against my back does nothing to calm the heat of frustration rising in my chest. I can't afford to let my personal life bleed into my work any more than it already has. But how do you compartmentalize your heart?

When I return to the OR, Ava glances up, her eyes meeting mine briefly before darting away. There's no room for weakness here, no space for the chaos inside me. But as I watch her steady hands, her focused expression, I wonder why she bothers. If she knew the mess my life is in, she'd run in the opposite direction.

I push through the rest of the day on autopilot, my mind a whirlwind of surgical steps and custody arguments. By the time I finish the last procedure, exhaustion weighs on me like lead. I retreat to my office, the door clicking shut behind me with a finality that echoes in the quiet space.

I drop into my chair and rub my temples, trying to fend off the headache that's been building all day. The photo of Lily on my desk catches my eye—her gap-toothed grin frozen in time. I pick it up, my thumb tracing the edges of the frame, lingering over the tiny smudges from her fingerprints. She deserves better than this tug-of-war between her parents.

A soft knock interrupts my thoughts. I glance up, expecting to see Linda or another nurse, but it's Ava. She hesitates in the doorway, her posture tense, as though she's unsure whether she's welcome.

"Dr. Cross? Do you have a moment?" Her voice is steady, but there's a flicker of uncertainty in her eyes.

I nod, gesturing for her to enter. She steps inside, closing the door behind her with a soft click. The room feels smaller suddenly, the air charged with an unspoken tension. "I wanted to apologize for yesterday," she begins, her gaze meeting mine directly. "I know I messed up, and I'm working on it. I won't let it happen again."

Her sincerity catches me off guard. I'm used to people placating me, offering hollow apologies to smooth over mistakes. But there's something different about Ava's words—a determination that mirrors my own when I was starting out.

"Mistakes happen," I say finally, surprising even myself with the lack of bite in my tone. "What matters is how you handle them moving forward."

Relief crosses her face, quickly replaced by that same determined focus I've seen in the OR. She nods, turning to leave, but pauses at the door.

"If you ever need an extra set of hands... or someone to talk to," she says quietly, "I'm around."

I watch her go, the door clicking shut behind her. Her words linger in the air, weaving through the cracks in my armor. Maybe, just maybe, I don't have to navigate this alone.

But even as I entertain the thought, my phone buzzes again.

Mark's name flashes across the screen, and my heart sinks.

"What now?" I mutter, answering the call.

"Ethan," Mark's voice is more urgent this time. "Your ex-wife's lawyer has new evidence— they're claiming you've been neglecting Lily's needs because of your job. There are pictures of you leaving the hospital late, and statements from neighbors about how rarely you're home."

I slam my fist against the desk, the sound reverberating through the room. "That's not neglect! I'm doing this for her—for her future!"

"I know, but the court might see it differently. We need to be proactive. Maybe consider reducing your hours… or showing more involvement in her daily life."

I stare at Lily's photo, the weight of Mark's words pressing down on me like an anchor. How do I balance being the best surgeon and the best father? Is it even possible?

The office feels suffocating. I stand abruptly, pacing the room, trying to find a solution that doesn't exist. The image of Ava's determined face flashes in my mind. Her offer echoes—"If you ever need someone to talk to…"

Maybe it's time I took someone up on that offer.

I pull out my phone, my thumb hesitating over the contacts list. For the first time in a long while, I consider reaching out—not as a surgeon or a colleague, but simply as a man trying to figure things out. But before I can press the call button, the office door opens again. This time, it's Linda, her expression a mix of urgency and concern.

"Dr. Cross, we need you back in the OR. Emergency case. Aortic dissection."

The weight on my chest tightens further, but I nod, tucking the phone back into my pocket. Duty calls, as it always does.

There is a life waiting to be saved.

Three

Surgical Interventions

To say I feel determined walking into the hospital today would be an understatement. Yesterday's disaster lingers in the back of my mind, but instead of dwelling on it, I let it fuel me. My start here might have been shaky, but I'm not about to let one bad day define me. Not when I've worked so hard to get here.

The hallways are buzzing with their usual morning rhythm—scrubs swishing, voices murmuring over charts, and monitors beeping in the distance. The sharp scent of antiseptic is almost comforting now. It reminds me that I'm in the thick of it, right where I want to be.

"Morning, Ava!" Linda greets me with her usual warm smile as I step into the nurse's station.

"Morning, Linda," I reply, injecting some pep into my voice.

15

"Ready for whatever comes my way today."

"That's the spirit," she says with a knowing wink. "There's a meeting in fifteen minutes. It might be a good chance to show your face."

A meeting. My stomach twists just a little. Meetings here are filled with doctors and senior nurses who've been at this hospital for years. Still, Linda's right. It's a chance to prove I'm serious about being part of this team.

The conference room is already half full when I arrive, and I slip into a chair near the back, trying to blend into the wall. The conversation buzzes around me—clinical protocols, staffing updates, equipment needs—but it's when the discussion turns to scrub nurse rotations that I tune in fully.

"Martinez is new, but she needs more shadowing before she can handle certain situations," one of the senior nurses says, her tone clipped and dismissive.

I shrink into my chair. Great. Another reminder that I'm at the bottom of the surgical food chain.

"I disagree." Ethan's voice cuts through the room. Calm, authoritative. All eyes turn toward him.

I blink in surprise, my breath catching.

"She handled herself well during yesterday's procedures. A few bumps are expected early on, but competence develops with

16

opportunity. Shadowing won't help if we don't let her step up."

My heart jumps into my throat. Did Ethan Cross just defend me?

The conversation moves on quickly to the next agenda item, but I'm left grappling with the weight of what just happened. Maybe I misjudged him.

* * *

Later that evening, I'm still thinking about his defense when chaos erupts. A "Code Rupture" call blares through the intercom, and suddenly the hospital is a flurry of activity.

"Emergency in OR 3!"

I race toward the OR, adrenaline spiking in my veins. A late-night emergency surgery is nothing unusual, but this one sound serious. When I step inside, Ethan is already there, scrubbing in with a calm intensity that belies the urgency of the situation.

"Martinez, you're scrubbing in," he says, barely glancing at me.

"Yes, Doctor," I reply, snapping on my gloves.

The room is a hive of movement and focus. The patient— a middle-aged man—is unconscious on the table, his vitals plummeting. The diagnosis: an abdominal aortic aneurysm. If we don't act fast, he'll bleed out right here on the table.

Ethan's voice is steady as he gives instructions. "We need to control the hemorrhaging before we go any further. Clamp."

I hand him the clamp, my fingers steady despite the chaos swirling around us. The sterile air is thick with tension, the hum of the machines almost deafening. My senses are on high alert— every movement calculated, every tool precise.

"Suction," Ethan says, his eyes never leaving the patient.

I move quickly, adjusting the suction tube as blood pools around the incision site. The clock on the wall ticks loudly in the background, each second feeling like a countdown. The patient's blood pressure drops further, and my heart races in response.

"Stay with me," Ethan murmurs, more to the patient than to anyone in the room. His voice is calm, but there's an edge of urgency that tightens the air.

The surgical team moves like a well-oiled machine. The anesthesiologist monitors the patient's vitals, calling out updates. The circulating nurse prepares additional instruments. Ethan works with a precision that borders on artistry, his hands steady and confident.

"Retractor," he says, and I place it in his hand without hesitation.

Minutes stretch into what feels like hours. Sweat beads at my temples, but I keep my focus razor-sharp. This is what I trained for. This is why I'm here.

"We're stabilizing," the anesthesiologist announces, and a collective breath seems to fill the room.

Ethan glances at me, a brief flicker of acknowledgment in his hazel eyes. "Good work, Martinez." "Thank you, Doctor," I manage, my voice steady despite the adrenaline still coursing through me.

* * *

Later, as I step into the elevator, exhausted from the night's intensity, I'm startled when Ethan slips in just before the doors close.

For a few moments, silence stretches between us. The air is thick with unspoken words, the weight of the surgery still pressing down on both of us.

Then, without warning, the elevator jolts violently.

I gasp, losing my balance. Ethan reaches for me at the same time I stumble forward, and suddenly, I'm against him—chest to chest, breath hitching. His hands steady me, gripping my waist with firm reassurance.

My heart pounds against my ribs. His scent—clean and sharp, like sterile soap and sandalwood, with a faint trace of something warm—fills my senses.

For a moment, neither of us moves. His face is inches from

mine, his breath mingling with mine in the confined space. My skin prickles under his touch, and I swear I see something flicker in his gaze—something just as charged as the electricity coursing through me.

The elevator steadies, but he doesn't let go immediately. His grip tightens for a fraction of a second, as if he's considering pulling me closer.

When he finally does let go, the moment shatters like glass.

"That was… unexpected," I murmur, forcing a breath into my lungs.

Ethan clears his throat, his fingers flexing before he shoves them into his pockets. "Yeah. You okay?"

I nod, though my body is still thrumming from the contact.

The elevator dings open, and we step out as if nothing happened. But something did. I can feel it in the way my skin still tingles where he touched me.

And I think, maybe, he feels it too.

* * *

Later that week, I'm walking past the pediatric unit when I spot him crouched beside a young patient—a little boy with wide, fearful eyes.

"It's okay, buddy," Ethan says gently. "We're just going to check your stitches, and then you'll be good to go."

The boy nods hesitantly, clutching a stuffed dinosaur.

Ethan's voice softens even more. "You like dinosaurs? Ethan's voice softens even more. "You like dinosaurs? Me too. Did you know the T. rex had tiny arms but could run really fast?"

The boy's eyes light up. "Really?"

"Really." Ethan grins, standing and ruffling the boy's hair before walking over to the nurse.

My heart squeezes unexpectedly. It's a side of Ethan I hadn't seen before—kind, patient, almost tender.

And as I watch him walk away, a mix of frustration and intrigue churns within me. One moment, he's defending my competence in a meeting; the next, he's distant and unreadable. The duality is maddening, yet I can't deny the pull I feel toward uncovering the layers beneath his stoic exterior.

But after that elevator moment... I have a feeling I'm not the only one struggling to keep the walls up.

Four

The Fault in Our Stars

The hospital hums with its usual blend of chaos and order. The steady beep of monitors, the whispered conversations between nurses, the hurried footsteps echoing down the corridors— it's a rhythm I've grown accustomed to. Predictable. Familiar. Safe.

Until today.

Because today, there's Ava Martinez.

I'm not sure exactly when she started occupying space in my thoughts. Maybe it was that night in the OR, when she held steady during a high-pressure emergency, her hands moving with precision despite the chaos swirling around her.

Or maybe it's the way she carries herself—bold but careful, determined yet composed.

Either way, it's a problem.

Because the last thing I need is a distraction.

And Ava? She's becoming impossible to ignore.

* * *

An Elevator, A Moment, and A Mistake Waiting to Happen

After another long shift, I step into the elevator, trying to roll the tension from my shoulders. The doors start to slide shut when I hear hurried footsteps echoing against the tile.

A hand thrusts between the metal doors, forcing them back open.

Ava.

She exhales a breath as she steps inside, brushing stray wisps of hair from her face. "Close one." I nod in acknowledgment, keeping my eyes fixed on the numbers above the door. Silence stretches between us, thick with something unspoken.

Then—the jolt.

A sharp, mechanical groan echoes through the small space. The floor lurches violently beneath us.

Ava stumbles.

Before I can think, my arms go around her just as she collides with my chest, her hands gripping my shoulders for balance.

The impact is sudden, but the reaction is worse.

She's warm. Too warm.

Close—too damn close.

I can feel the press of her body against mine, the soft hitch of her breath against my neck. The faintest trace of her scent—something warm and subtly sweet, like vanilla and rain—lingers between us, filling my senses.

I should step back. I should let go immediately.

Instead, I don't move.

For a split second, the world narrows down to the small, steel box and the space between us. No distractions, no responsibilities, no custody battles—just this.

Her lips part slightly, her breath ghosting over mine.

Damn it.

Then, with a jarring lurch, the elevator resumes its descent, the moment shattering between us like dropped glass.

Ava clears her throat, stepping back quickly as if trying to regain control. "That was... unexpected."

Understatement of the year.

I inhale deeply through my nose, forcing my pulse to slow, and loosen my grip on her arms. "Yeah. You okay?"

She nods, though there's a pink flush high on her cheeks. I don't let myself dwell on how good that color looks on her.

The elevator dings. The doors slide open to the bustling hallway. Just like that, it's over.

We step out, walking in opposite directions, but the tension? It lingers.

And no matter how hard I try, I can't shake the phantom feeling of her body pressed against mine.

* * *

Everywhere I Turn, There She Is

The moment follows me for the rest of the night, searing like a brand against my skin. And the worst part? Ava is everywhere.

In the OR, handing off instruments with steady precision, her focus unwavering.

In pediatrics, kneeling beside a young patient, making balloon animals out of surgical gloves to distract him from the pain.

At the nurse's station, laughing softly at something Linda said, her expression light and unguarded.

Every time, I tell myself not to look.

But I do.

And every damn time, I remember the way she felt against me.

I'm standing in the break room later, sipping a terrible excuse for coffee, when I hear her voice. "Hey, Dr. Cross."

Ava.

She steps up beside me at the counter, her own cup in hand. The space between us feels smaller than it should, charged with static.

"Martinez," I acknowledge, keeping my tone carefully neutral.

"Busy day?"

I nod. "Always."

She shifts slightly, as if debating something, then says, "I saw you with that little boy in pediatrics earlier. You're good with

26

kids."

My shoulders tense slightly. Most people don't notice things like that—or they don't care to look past the surgeon to the man.

I roll my shoulders, keeping my expression unreadable. "I like kids. They're easier to reason with than adults."

Ava lets out a small laugh. "I don't know. Kids can be pretty stubborn."

I smirk, but I don't say anything else.

I can feel her watching me, searching for something beneath the surface. I refuse to give her anything.

The barista calls my name, and I take my coffee, nodding briefly. "See you around, Martinez."

And with that, I walk away.

Because whatever this is between us?

It's a distraction I can't afford.

But that doesn't mean I don't feel her watching me as I leave.

* * *

A Late Night, A Rooftop, and a Line We Can't Cross

It's well past midnight when I find myself on the hospital's rooftop garden, the quiet hum of the city stretching beneath me.

The cold air clears my head, giving me the space I need to shake off the weight of the day.

Then—footsteps.

I don't have to turn around to know who it is.

"You always come up here this late?" Ava asks, stepping up beside the railing.

I glance at her. "I could ask you the same thing."

She smiles, wrapping her arms around herself for warmth against the night chill. "It's the best place to think."

We fall into silence, the distant sounds of traffic filling the gaps between us.

Then, quietly, she says, "For the record, you're wrong about kids being easier than adults."

I arch a brow, turning to face her. "That so?"

She nods. "Adults at least pretend to follow logic. Kids? They

28

do whatever they want. No filter. No hesitation."

I smirk. "That's exactly why they're easier."

She turns to face me fully. "So, what, you like that they don't pretend?"

I pause, considering her words. Then, surprising even myself with the honesty, I say, "Yeah. I do."

She watches me for a long moment, something curious and searching in her gaze.

I should look away.

I should end this conversation right now.

Instead, I let the silence stretch between us, heavy with everything we aren't saying.

Ava shifts slightly, her shoulder almost brushing mine.

And for the second time today, I have the sudden, dangerous urge to close the space between us.

Instead, I step back.

I see the flicker of something in her expression—disappointment, maybe.

I clear my throat. "You should get some sleep, Martinez."

She exhales, then gives me a small nod. "Yeah. You too."

She turns to leave.

And I let her go.

Because if I don't?

I won't be able to stop myself

* * *

The Unraveling

The next few days pass in a blur of surgeries and consultations, but the tension?

It doesn't fade.

Ava Martinez has become an unexpected variable in my carefully controlled world, and for the first time in a long time, I don't know how to handle it.

I tell myself it's nothing.

I tell myself it doesn't matter. But every time I see her—

I feel it.

And that—more than anything—terrifies me.

Five

Boundaries and Bandages

The hospital feels different today.

It's not the usual chaos of beeping monitors, urgent footsteps, and rushed conversations. It's something else entirely.

Like a shift in gravity. A current running just beneath the surface, unseen but undeniably there.

I blame Ethan Cross.

He's been occupying my thoughts more than I care to admit. Not just his presence, but his contradictions.

The way he's all sharp edges and ice in the OR but unexpectedly gentle with patients.

The way he holds himself apart, yet sometimes, for a fleeting second, lets his guard drop. The way he looked at me when the elevator jolted, his arms locked around me, as if the whole damn hospital had disappeared and we were the only two people left in the world.

I shake my head, exhaling sharply. *Get it together, Ava.*

* * *

Later That Day – A Coffee Break That's Not So Simple

The break room is nearly empty when I step inside, needing caffeine like my life depends on it. I make a beeline for the coffee machine, pouring myself a cup, only to realize—

I'm not alone.

Ethan.

He's sitting at one of the small round tables, long legs stretched out, shoulders heavy with exhaustion. His head is tilted downward, his eyes locked on his phone. The dark shadows beneath them tell me he's running on next to no sleep.

I should walk away. I should give him space.

Instead, I grab a chair across from him. "You look like you're contemplating a career change."

He exhales a tired laugh, running a hand over his face. "Tempting. What do you think? Professional fisherman? Coffee shop owner?"

I pretend to consider the options. "Fisherman? No chance. You don't strike me as the patient type."

His brow lifts slightly. "And coffee shop owner?"

"Well," I smirk, "if your skills in surgery translate to making lattes, then maybe. But I have my doubts."

He huffs a laugh, shaking his head. "For the record, I make excellent coffee."

I lean forward, intrigued. "Oh? Big claim. Ever actually worked a barista shift?"

"No," he admits, setting his phone down on the table. "But I've survived hospital coffee for over a decade. You learn survival skills."

I snort. "Okay, Dr. Cross. I'll believe it when I taste it."

His lips quirk, the tension in his features easing for just a moment.

It's dangerous, how easy this is.

How easy it would be to forget that there are lines we shouldn't cross.

I shake off the thought and take a sip of my coffee—only to gag immediately.

Ethan watches with mild amusement as I cough into my sleeve. "Yeah," he says, completely unfazed. "Hospital sludge. You should know better by now."

I glare at him over the rim of the cup. "Why didn't you warn me?"

He shrugs, completely unapologetic. "It was more entertaining this way."

He's still smirking when his phone buzzes again, his amusement fading in an instant.

His shoulders go rigid, his expression shutting down completely. "Everything okay?" I ask before I can stop myself.

He hesitates, then sighs, pocketing his phone. "Court stuff." I don't press.

I don't need to. The rumors around the hospital aren't subtle—whispers of an ugly custody battle, legal fees stacking up, a little girl stuck in the middle.

"I'm sure it's overwhelming," I say softly.

He exhales, rubbing a hand across his jaw. "That's an understatement."

For a moment, there's nothing but the low hum of the vending machine and the distant murmur of voices outside in the hall.

Then, on impulse, I push the coffee cup toward him. "Here. You can have the rest of this abomination as a peace offering."

He huffs a quiet laugh but takes it. "How generous of you."

I grin. "I'm practically a saint."

Something shifts in his expression—just for a second.

Something warm. Something I don't trust myself to name.

He lifts the cup, taking a cautious sip. He grimaces. "Yeah. This is terrible."

I burst out laughing. And for just a moment, nothing else exists.

Not the stress of our jobs. Not the lines we're dangerously close to crossing.

Not the custody battle looming over him.

Just this.

Just us.

* * *

That Night – The Charity Auction

The hospital's annual charity auction is one of the biggest events of the year. Every department gets involved, and a staggering amount of money is raised for pediatric research.

I hadn't planned on going.

But Linda volunteered me, so now I'm here, standing at the back of the hospital's ballroom, wearing a silk dress that doesn't feel like mine.

The space is buzzing with conversation. Guests in evening wear mingle over champagne, their laughter echoing through the towering ceilings.

I scan the crowd, checking last-minute auction details on my clipboard, when a familiar voice speaks right behind me.

"You're late."

I turn—

And nearly forget how to breathe.

Ethan stands there in a perfectly tailored suit, his shirt unbuttoned at the collar, sleeves pushed up slightly—like he was ready to be formal but got tired of the effort halfway through.

It's frankly unfair how good he looks.

I arch a brow, recovering my composure. "I wasn't aware I was on your schedule."

He smirks. "You're on everyone's schedule. This event would fall apart without you."

I laugh, shaking my head. "Flattery, Dr. Cross? Are you feeling okay?"

He chuckles, but there's something else in his expression—something quieter. Something unreadable.

Then, before I can dwell on it, the auctioneer takes the stage, signaling the start of the event.

* * *

Later – The Balcony

After the last of the guests trickle out, I escape to the balcony, the cool night air a relief against my skin.

The city stretches before me, twinkling lights blurring into the horizon.

I close my eyes. Exhale.

Then—footsteps.

"You hiding?"

I glance over my shoulder.

Ethan.

Tie loosened, glass of whiskey in hand, leaning against the railing like he owns the night.

"Just… catching my breath," I admit.

He nods, stepping closer. "Not bad for a night's work."

I let out a soft laugh. "Yeah. Not bad at all."

For a moment, we just stand there, the air charged, humming with something unspoken.

I can feel him watching me, the weight of his gaze heavy in the stillness.He shifts slightly, his shoulder nearly brushing mine.

"I—" he starts. Then stops. I turn to him fully. "What?"

His jaw tightens, and for a moment, I think he's going to say something important.

Instead, he shakes his head. "Nothing."

But it's not nothing. It's everything.

The hesitation. The wanting.

The unspoken question hanging between us, unanswered.

And as we walk back inside, side by side, I know one thing for certain.

Whatever this thing is between us? I

t's only getting harder to ignore.

Six

Heart Transplants

⁘

The hospital is supposed to be the one place where I have control. A place where skill outweighs emotion, where precision silences chaos. But lately, that control is slipping.

And it has everything to do with Ava Martinez.

Last night's charity auction was supposed to be just another hospital event—smiling at donors, shaking hands, making sure the evening didn't devolve into a disaster. Instead, it turned into something else entirely.

It was the way Ava looked in that black dress, standing under the ballroom lights like she belonged there—elegant, confident. It was the way we kept ending up next to each other, the way every conversation between us felt like a challenge, a dance neither of us wanted to admit we were leading.

41

But it was the balcony that really got me.

The way she looked out at the city, lost in thought, her guard down in a way I'd rarely seen before. The way I almost told her something real, something I never let slip to anyone.

I didn't, of course.

Because I can't.

Because this thing between us? It's getting dangerously close to something I can't afford right now.

Because I know what's coming. And the moment I let myself want her is the moment I risk losing everything.

* * *

Inside the OR

Surgery is the only thing that keeps my head clear. One cut. One clamp. One stitch at a time. It's all I need to focus on.

But as I scrub in for a heart transplant the next morning, Ava is already there, gloving up, her expression sharp with focus.

And suddenly, all I can think about is last night.

Her laugh. The way she teased me over the terrible hospital

coffee. The way she fit so perfectly next to me on the balcony.

I need to shut this down.

But then she meets my gaze, and just like that, the rest of the world fades into the background.

Damn it.

The patient is stable, for now. But there's no room for error.

"We need to move fast," I say, my voice steady.

"Ready when you are," Ava replies, placing the scalpel in my hand without hesitation.

For the next several hours, it's just us—a team, locked into the rhythm of surgery. Every movement is precise, every instruction followed before I even have to say it. She anticipates what I need before I do, and I don't have time to figure out why that gets under my skin.

She belongs here. I knew it before, but now I feel it in my bones.

The heart beats. The patient stabilizes. It's a win.

I glance at Ava as we step back from the table, exhaustion settling into my shoulders. She's looking at me with something unreadable in her eyes, something that makes my pulse slow just slightly.

"Nice work, Martinez," I say, keeping my tone neutral.

She gives me a small, tired smile. "Same to you, Dr. Cross."

But the weight of the moment lingers long after we leave the OR.

* * *

After the Surgery

I should go to my office. Should review the case notes for my next surgery. Should do literally anything except this.

But instead, I find myself walking to the break room, knowing exactly who I'll find.

Ava is sitting at the table, stirring a terrible cup of hospital coffee. She looks up when I step inside, arching an eyebrow. "Don't tell me you came to challenge me to another round of *Operation*."

I smirk, remembering our ridiculous game night in the break room a few days ago. The way she goaded me into playing. The way I lost—which I will never admit was on purpose.

"I think I've suffered enough humiliation for one week," I say, grabbing a cup of coffee that I know I won't drink.

Ava grins. "So you're admitting defeat?"

I scoff. "I'm allowing you to believe you won."

She leans forward slightly, eyes sparkling with amusement. "That's a very polite way of saying you lost."

I shake my head, but I can't stop the corner of my mouth from lifting.

This. This is the problem.

Because Ava makes it too damn easy.

For a few minutes, the weight of court dates and custody battles and legal threats doesn't exist. It's just her and me. Teasing, talking, existing.

And I don't realize how badly I've needed that until now.

* * *

The Courthouse Call

The walls of the hospital usually feel safe, but today they feel suffocating, the air too thick with tension.

Every time I sit across from my lawyer, it's another battle. Another hurdle in a war I can't afford to lose. I'm walking to my car when my phone rings, pulling me from my thoughts.

"Ethan," my lawyer says, his tone grim. "We need to talk. There are new allegations. Serious ones. We're going to have to escalate our defense."

The world tilts slightly, and my breath catches in my throat.

"How bad?" I ask, my voice lower now.

"Bad," he confirms. "Meet me at the office as soon as you can."

I end the call, gripping the edge of my car door, trying to force air back into my lungs.

This was already an uphill battle. But if they're pulling this, if they're making me out to be something I'm not, then—

Then I could lose her.

Lily.

My daughter. My whole damn world.

The weight is unbearable, pressing down until I can barely breathe.

My hand hovers over my phone, my fingers itching to text Ava.

To hear her voice, to get a moment of steadiness, of clarity, before I walk into this next fight.

But I can't.

Because if I pull her into this, I risk making her a target too.

So instead, I shove the phone in my pocket and get in the car, my hands tightening on the wheel as the city blurs around me.

* * *

The Message That Changes Everything

I'm halfway home when my phone buzzes again.

Expecting my lawyer, I glance at the screen—

It's not him.

It's a photo.

A grainy, low-light image of me and Ava on the hospital rooftop, laughing, coffee cups in hand. It looks intimate. It looks damning.

The message attached is short, sharp, and loaded with implication:

Think the court will like this?

My blood runs cold.

Before I can process the full weight of what it means, another message pings through:

More where that came from.

The light ahead turns green, but I don't move.

I'm frozen, trapped between the life I've built and the storm that's about to tear it apart.

Because I know exactly what this means.

They're going after Ava now.

And for the first time, I don't know how to fight back

Seven

The Scrubbed-In Miracle

Some days in the hospital blur together—the hum of machines, the hurried steps in the hallways, the constant rhythm of saving lives.

But today isn't one of those days.

Today, everything feels different.

I feel it in the way my fingers hover over the door handle of the nurse's station, in the way my heart won't settle in my chest.

Something is shifting—I just don't know what yet.

And I have a feeling it has everything to do with Ethan Cross.

* * *

A Conversation We Can't Ignore

"Dr. Cross is looking for you," Linda says casually, handing me a patient chart.

My fingers tighten around the folder. Of course, he is.

"Oh?" I say, trying—and failing—to keep my voice neutral.

Linda smirks, but she doesn't say anything else. She doesn't have to. She's been watching, throwing me those knowing glances ever since the charity auction.

I push away the nerves and head toward the observation room, where I know he'll be.

Where he always is when something is weighing on him.

When I step inside, he's exactly where I expect—standing by the wide glass window, overlooking the OR floor below. His shoulders are tense, his posture unyielding and rigid.

Something is wrong.

"Ethan?" I call softly.

He turns at the sound of my voice, and for just a second, his expression softens. But whatever emotion flickers in his hazel eyes is quickly masked by something heavier.

Something that makes my stomach drop.

"We need to talk," he says, his voice low but steady.

A knot tightens in my chest. That's never a good sign.

"What's going on?" I ask, stepping fully into the room and letting the door click shut behind me.

Ethan exhales, running a hand over his face. "There's been a new development in the custody case. It's worse than I expected."

I take a step closer. "What happened?"

"The other side's lawyers are pulling every dirty trick they can." His voice is edged with frustration. "They're trying to use my schedule against me, saying I work too much, that I can't be a stable parent."

"That's ridiculous," I snap. "You're an amazing father."

His jaw clenches, but then he hesitates—as if that's not the worst of it.

I narrow my eyes. "There's more, isn't there?"

His throat works before he finally says it.

"They're using us."

The word hits like a physical punch to the chest.

"Us?" I echo, my pulse spiking.

He nods grimly. "Someone sent photos to the court. Of us talking on the rooftop. Laughing. Having coffee. They're twisting it—trying to make it look like I'm… distracted. That I'm prioritizing a relationship over my daughter."

My stomach churns with anger. "That's insane! You've done nothing but fight for her. How could they—"

"It doesn't matter," he interrupts, his voice hardening. "Not in court. They don't care about the truth. They care about how it looks."

I grip the ledge of the observation window behind me, my fingers pressing into the cold surface.

This isn't fair.

Ethan is one of the most disciplined, dedicated people I've ever met. He has sacrificed everything for his daughter.

And now, they're trying to weaponize something that isn't even real—something we haven't even let ourselves acknowledge.

Until now.

"We'll figure this out," I say, stepping closer until I'm standing right in front of him. "They're not going to win. You're fighting for the right reasons. That has to count for something."

For a moment, he just looks at me, something unreadable in his gaze.

Then, so softly I almost miss it, he murmurs, "Thank you."

The air between us thickens.

There's something unspoken, something I can't quite name. It crackles in the space between us, dangerous and inevitable.

Before I can second-guess myself, my hand moves—fingertips grazing his forearm.

Ethan glances at where I've touched him, his breath shallow, his chest rising and falling in a rhythm that matches mine.

"Ava," he says, my name sounding almost like a warning.

I know what he's going to say.

We can't.

But I don't step back. And neither does he.

I should.

We should.

Instead, my body betrays me. I tilt my chin up, my lips parting, my pulse hammering against my ribs.

And that's all it takes.

Slowly, hesitantly, he leans in.

His lips graze mine, tentative at first, as if he's waiting for me to pull away.

I don't pull away.

The kiss is soft, almost fragile, but it's filled with everything we haven't been saying—the stolen glances, the lingering touches, the tension that's been building since the moment we met.

When we finally break apart, he rests his forehead against mine, his breath uneven.

"I've wanted to do that for a while," he admits, his voice barely more than a whisper.

I let out a shaky laugh. "Me too."

For the first time in months, the weight on my chest eases.

Maybe, just maybe, we're stronger together than apart.

* * *

The Rooftop Confession

That night, I find myself back on the rooftop.

The city stretches before me, the lights twinkling in the distance. But all I can think about is Ethan.

And the fact that we finally—finally—crossed a line we can't erase.

I care about him. More than I should.

More than I ever intended to.

I've spent years keeping people at arm's length, building walls so high that no one could get in.

And somehow, Ethan Cross slipped through them without me even realizing it.

My phone buzzes in my pocket.

It's a message from him.

You were right. I needed to hear that. Thank you.

Warmth spreads through me, and before I can talk myself out of it, I type back:

Anytime. You've got this.

55

It feels like such a small thing.

But I know better.

This?

This isn't small at all.

* * *

The Verdict

The next morning, the hospital is buzzing with activity, but I can't focus on anything.

Ethan's custody hearing is today.

And I'm not there.

I told myself I wouldn't be—that it's not my place.

But that doesn't stop me from checking my phone every five minutes, waiting for a message that doesn't come.

By the time my shift ends, I feel raw with nerves.

Then, just as I'm leaving the hospital, my phone rings.

I answer immediately. "Ethan?"

There's a long pause.

Then, finally—

"I won."

The relief that floods through me is instant. "Ethan, that's amazing!"

I can hear the disbelief in his voice. Like he still can't believe it's over.

"Can I see you?" he asksI don't hesitate.

"Of course."

* * *

The Café

He's already waiting when I arrive.

And for the first time in weeks, he looks lighter.

We sit across from each other, the noise of the café fading into something distant.

"This isn't just about custody," he says after a long moment. "It's about starting over."

He holds my gaze, something certain and steady in his expression.

"For me, for Lily… for us."

My heart stutters.

"Us?" I whisper.

His fingers brush mine across the table. "If you'll have me."

A million thoughts race through my mind.

And yet—

Only one matters.

"Yes," I breathe.

And when he smiles, slow and sure, I know—

I wouldn't have chosen anything else

Eight

The Future We Choose

Winning custody of Lily was supposed to be the hardest battle of my life.

But sitting across from Ava at the café, watching the way her eyes search mine, I realize that choosing what comes next is just as terrifying.

And just as important.

* * *

A Moment of Clarity

She's waiting at our usual table, a coffee cup cradled in her hands. She looks up as I approach, and when our gazes meet, something inside me finally settles.

She smiles—soft, expectant, hopeful—and for the first time in months, I don't feel like I have to fight for something to be mine.

"I want to start over," I say, taking the seat opposite her.

Her brow furrows slightly. "What do you mean?"

"With you. With Lily. With life." I lean forward, resting my forearms on the table, needing her to understand. "I don't want to just win custody. I want to build something real—for her. And for me."

Ava studies me, her fingers tracing the rim of her cup. She's always been good at reading between the lines, knowing what I mean even when I don't say it outright.

She tilts her head. "And where do I fit into this picture?"

The question is quiet, hesitant, but laced with a vulnerability that tugs at my chest.

I don't hesitate. "Right in the middle of it."

A flicker of emotion crosses her face. Surprise. Maybe

something more.

Slowly, she reaches across the table, her fingertips brushing mine. "Then let's start over."

It's a simple statement. But it means everything.

* * *

The First Step

Introducing Ava to Lily isn't just something I want—it's something I need.

If this is going to work, if this is going to be real, then the two people who mean the most to me have to meet each other where it matters.

We decide on the park, a neutral ground where Lily can just be herself—and where Ava can see her the way I do.

When we arrive, Lily is already climbing the jungle gym, her laughter ringing through the air. Ava fidgets beside me, nervous in a way I've never seen before.

I smirk. "Relax."

She glares at me. "You relax. I don't want to mess this up."

"You won't," I promise, nudging her lightly with my shoulder.

She exhales a long breath. "I hope you're right."

Lily finally notices us and bounds over, skidding to a stop in the mulch when she sees Ava. She stares, her small arms crossing over her chest as she assesses the situation with a scrutiny that mirrors my own.

"Lily," I say, crouching down to her level. "This is my friend, Ava."

She doesn't say anything at first, her eyes narrowing slightly. "The one from the pictures?"

Ava's eyes widen. "Pictures?"

I sigh, rubbing the back of my neck. "She's been eavesdropping when she should have been sleeping."

Lily shrugs, completely unbothered by the accusation. "It's true."

Ava bites her lip, trying not to laugh. "Well, since you already know me, I guess we should be friends."

Lily studies her for another second, then sticks out her hand like a tiny business executive closing a deal. "Okay. But I get to pick the game."

Ava shakes her hand, looking genuinely relieved. "Deal."

Just like that, she's part of Lily's world.And part of mine.

* * *

A Late-Night Confession

That night, after Lily is tucked into bed, Ava and I sit on my apartment's balcony, watching the city lights flicker in the distance.

She's quiet, her gaze focused on the horizon. I can tell she's thinking, processing, wondering what comes next.

"You okay?" I ask.

She nods. "Yeah. Just… it's a lot."

I rest my elbow on the chair's armrest, studying her profile in the moonlight. "Second thoughts?"

She turns her head toward me, her eyes warm and sure. "Not even a little."

Something tight in my chest finally eases.

"Good," I murmur, reaching for her hand. "Because I meant what I said earlier. About this being a fresh start."

Ava threads her fingers with mine, squeezing lightly. "So did I."

The words feel bigger than just a conversation.

They feel like a promise.

* * *

Six Months Later

Life doesn't always change overnight, but it shifts in the small moments.

Mornings with Lily, making pancakes even though she insists on putting way too much syrup on them. Late-night shifts at the hospital where I pass Ava in the hallway and smirk just to get a reaction out of her.

Evenings spent on the couch, her head on my shoulder, Lily tucked under my arm, a terrible animated movie playing in the background.

It's good.

Better than I ever let myself imagine.

At work, Ava and I have fallen into an easy rhythm. She's the only one who challenges me without hesitation, who calls me out when I need it, but always has my back when it counts.

One afternoon, I walk up behind her at the nurse's station,

glancing over her shoulder. "Reading patient notes like they're a murder mystery again?"

She doesn't even flinch. "If I find a plot twist, I'll let you know."

I smirk. "You're supposed to be working."

She turns toward me, one eyebrow raised. "You're not supposed to be annoying me, and yet, here we are."

I chuckle, leaning against the counter. "You love it."

Linda, passing by with a clipboard, sighs dramatically. "I swear, the tension between you two was exhausting before you got together. But now? Somehow worse."

Ava chokes on her coffee. "Linda!"

I just smirk. "She's not wrong."

Ava glares at me. "You are the absolute worst."

I lean in slightly, just to mess with her. "You love that too."

She opens her mouth to argue, then shuts it, sighing heavily. "I hate that you're right."

Linda snorts. "Took her long enough to admit it."

Ava groans, muttering something under her breath. But I see the way she fights a smile.

65

This?

This is home.

* * *

An Unspoken Future

That night, back at the apartment, Lily is sprawled across the floor, building something out of Legos with a level of intensity usually reserved for bomb disposal.

Ava sits beside me on the couch, one of my old t-shirts hanging off her shoulder, her bare feet tucked under her legs. She's reading, but I can tell she's not really focused.

After a while, she finally closes the book and looks over at me.

"Do you ever think about what's next?" she asks.

I glance at her. "Next?"

She nods, shifting slightly. "After this. After the hospital. After... all of it."

I exhale, considering the question.

And then I say the only thing that's ever felt completely certain.

"I don't care what's next." I lace my fingers with hers, running my thumb over her knuckles. "As long as you're in it."

Ava's breath catches, and then she smiles—slow and sure and steady.

"I think I can promise that," she whispers.

Lily, without looking up from her plastic bricks, groans dramatically. "Are you guys being mushy again?"

Ava grins. "Obviously."

Lily sighs, shaking her head. "Okay. But can we please do that after I finish my castle?"

Ava laughs. "Absolutely."

Lily nods, satisfied, before returning to her masterpiece.

I glance at Ava. And in that moment, I know—

This isn't just something temporary.

This is the life I fought for.

And I wouldn't change a single second of it